P9-DSY-777

HAMILTON EAST

j CHAPTER BK Aquaman
Mason, Jane B.
  Black Manta and the octopus army
                                1|14

9781434238986 (pbk.)

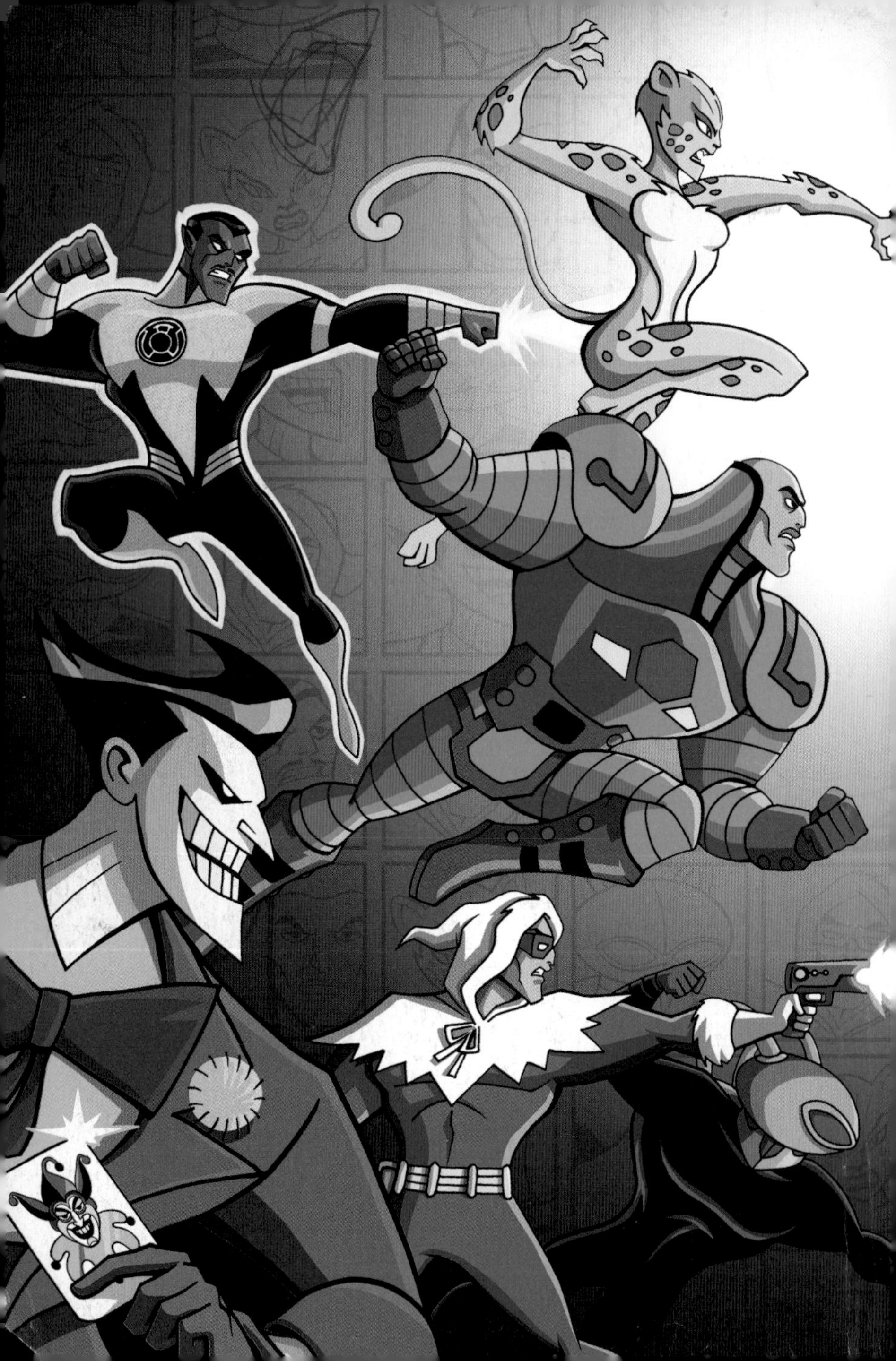

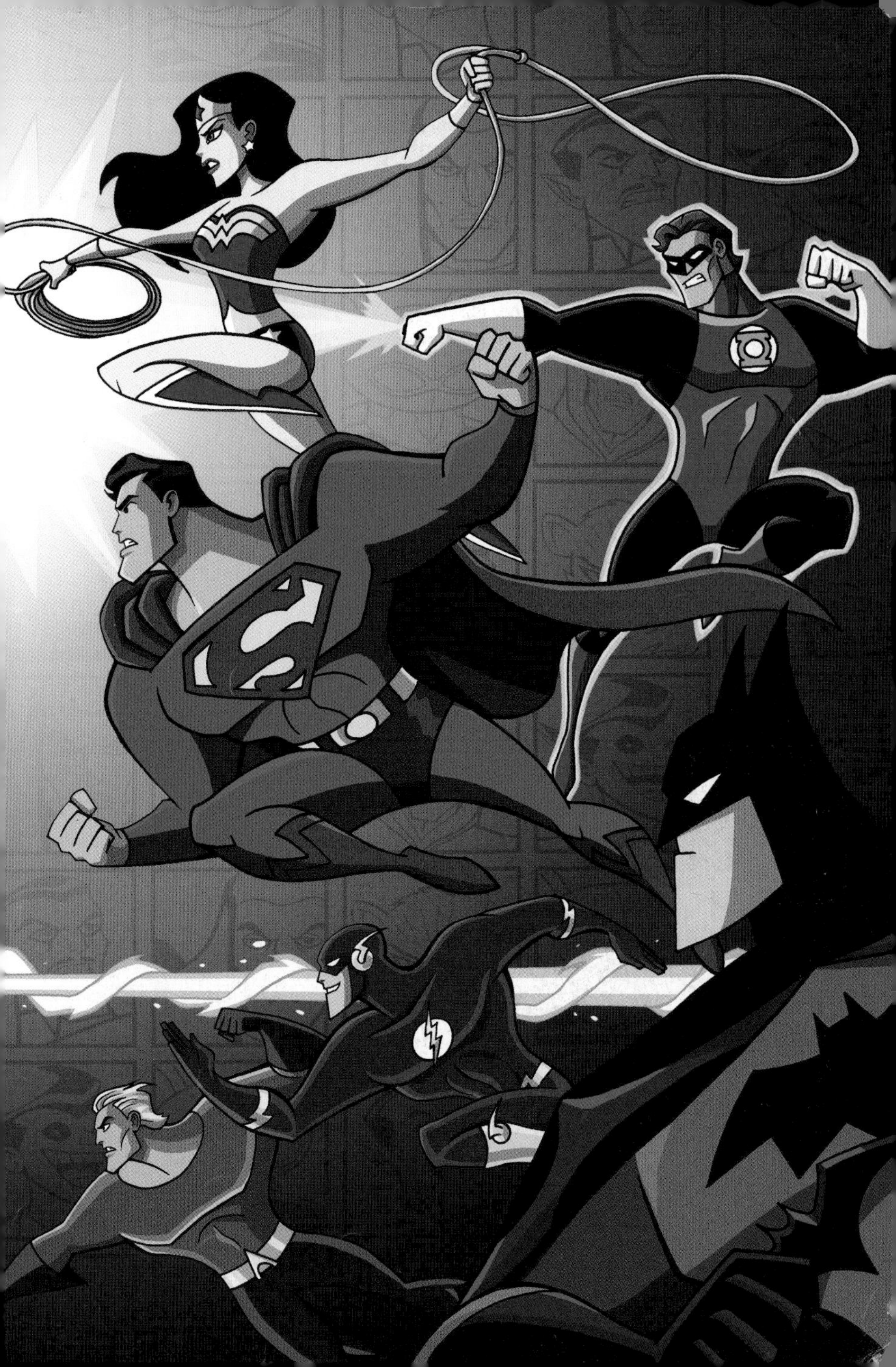

SUPER DC HEROES VILLAINS

BLACK MANTA AND THE OCTOPUS ARMY

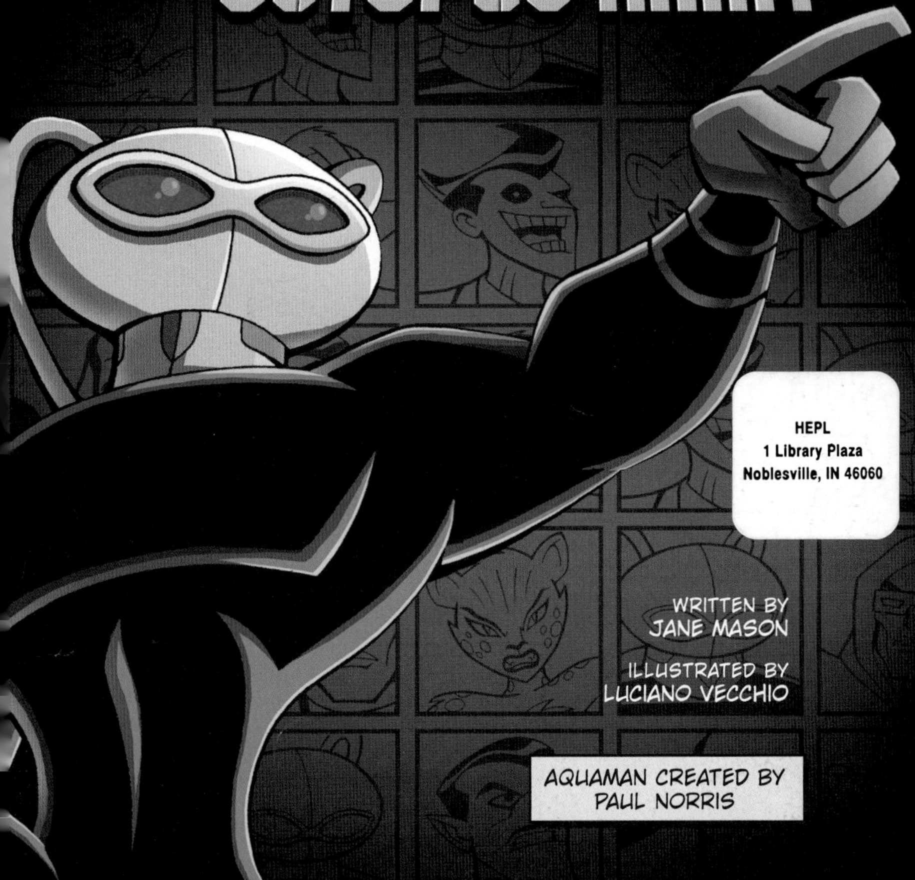

WRITTEN BY
JANE MASON

ILLUSTRATED BY
LUCIANO VECCHIO

AQUAMAN CREATED BY
PAUL NORRIS

STONE ARCH BOOKS
a capstone imprint

Published by Stone Arch Books in 2012
A Capstone Imprint
1710 Roe Crest Drive
North Mankato, MN 56003
www.capstonepub.com

Copyright © 2012 DC Comics.
BLACK MANTA and all related characters and
elements are trademarks of and © DC Comics.
(s12)

STAR25083

No part of this publication may be reproduced
in whole or in part, or stored in a retrieval
system, or transmitted in any form or by any
means, electronic, mechanical, photocopying,
recording, or otherwise, without written
permission.

Cataloging-in-Publication Data is available at
the Library of Congress website

ISBN: 978-1-4342-3797-2 (library binding)
ISBN: 978-1-4342-3898-6 (paperback)

Summary: The deep-sea super-villain Black
Manta is out to destroy Atlantis once and
for all! He's engineered an army of evil octopi
to crush the underwater city and destroy its
heroic ruler, Aquaman. If the Sea King can't
stop the underwater marauder and his squid
soldiers, Atlantis could be lost again!

Printed in the United States of America in Stevens Point,
Wisconsin.
102011
006404WZS12

TABLE OF CONTENTS

BLACK MANTA

REAL NAME: Unknown

OCCUPATION: Assassin

HEIGHT: 6' 4"

WEIGHT: 250 lbs.

EYES: Brown

HAIR: Brown

BIOGRAPHY:

Before Black Manta became a super-villain, he was a young boy with a severe illness. His only comfort . . . the sea. Then one day, while playing in the ocean, the boy was kidnapped and imprisoned on a small ship. After several years of harsh treatment by his captors, the boy spotted hope on the horizon — Aquaman. The boy called out, but the Sea King did not hear him. At that moment, he vowed revenge against Aquaman. After escaping the ship, he designed a high-tech, submersible costume and took the name Black Manta, devil of the deep.

Power Helmet

Infrared Vision

High-tech Uniform

Jet Boots

Wrist Gauntle-

POWERS/ABILITIES:
Possesses above-average
strength; quickly masters
new equipment; fueled by
extreme rage.

CHAPTER 1

UNDERSEA SOLDIERS

Black Manta's red eyes glowed. In a secret hideout beneath the seafloor, the super-villain studied hundreds of octopuses trapped inside high-tech tanks. He smiled behind his alien-like helmet. No one knew about his latest creations, but they would soon find out.

Each octopus was part of his brilliant scheme to conquer the underwater city of Atlantis and defeat its king, Aquaman, once and for all! And so far, Black Manta's plan was coming along perfectly.

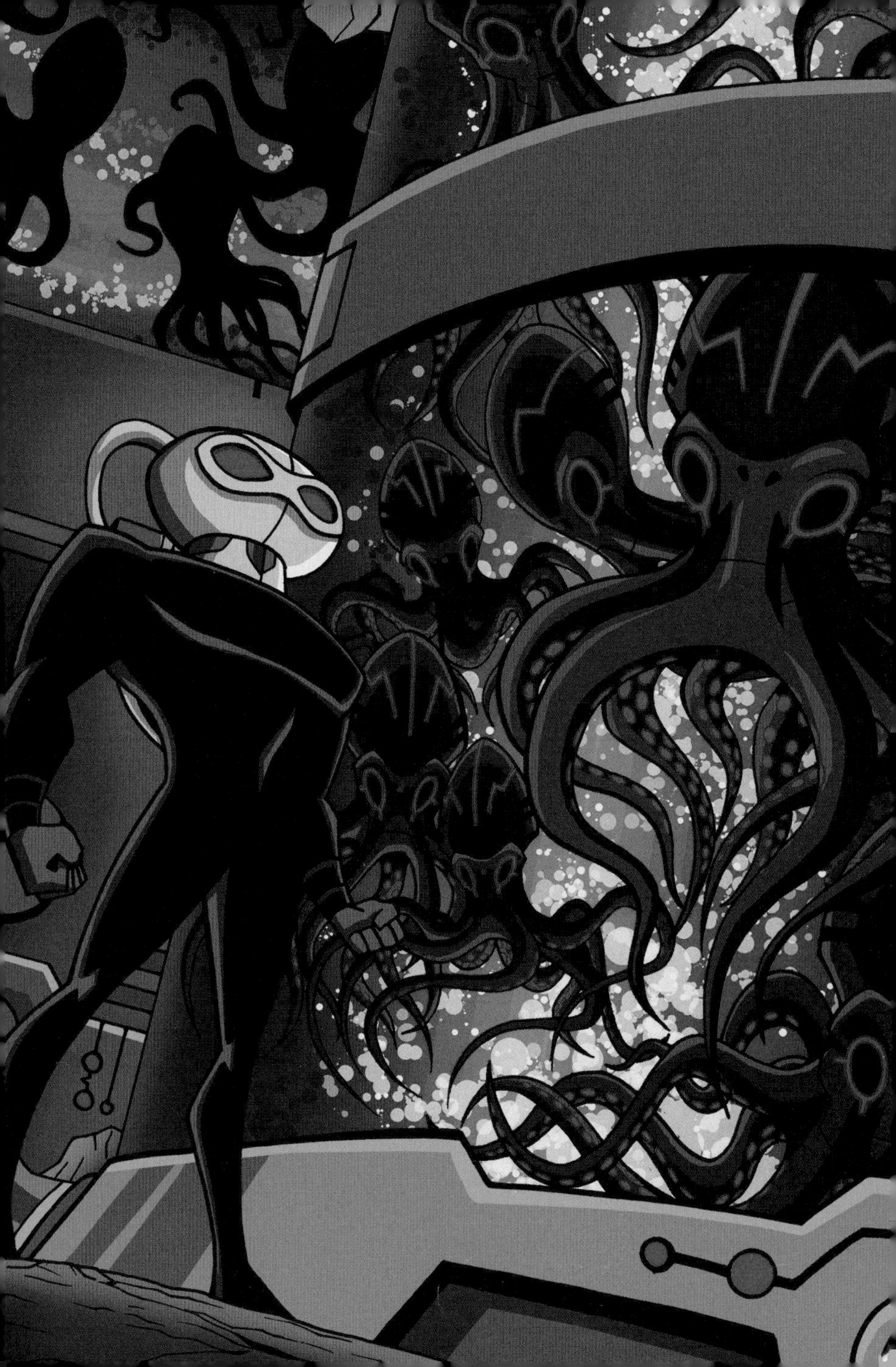

For years, he had searched the darkest depths of the ocean, seeking soldiers for his army. Finally, he discovered the perfect specimens for his plan — giant octopuses. These eight-tentacled beasts had everything the super-villain was looking for, including unmatched intelligence and amazing speed. These traits also made them difficult creatures to capture and recruit. Black Manta, however, loved a challenge.

First, the super-villain created a device to speak with the sea creatures. Then, using nets, he captured hundreds of octopuses and placed them in saltwater tanks. The tanks took up an entire wing of the massive hideout he had carved out of the seafloor, just outside the city limits of Atlantis. Of course, Black Manta didn't use the word "prison" when he spoke to his octopuses.

The super-villain used words like "comfortable" and "new" and "home." He told the sea creatures that he was their friend, that together they made a very good team, and that they would rule the seas! And he fed them the freshest fish, clams, and crabs he could find.

Black Manta pressed the button on his communicator and pointed it at the octopuses. They wriggled excitedly, waiting for him to speak. After months of training, they considered him their master, their leader. They obeyed his every command.

That was good, because if he was going to succeed the octopuses needed to obey him at all costs. And Black Manta had every intention of succeeding.

The super-villain had hated the Sea King for as long as he could remember.

This hatred had begun when Aquaman ignored a young boy's cries for help. The boy was imprisoned on a ship, and his captors were not kind. They made the boy work all day, didn't feed him enough food, and he barely slept. This treatment went on for months, for years.

When the boy saw Aquaman swimming nearby, he was sure he'd be saved. He shouted and waved his arms excitedly. He called the hero's name again and again, but Aquaman just swam away.

That day, the boy took matters into his own young hands. He vowed to be free. He vowed to seek revenge on Aquaman and to one day rule the seas.

Eventually, that boy escaped his captors. In order to survive in the sea, he had to find a way to breathe underwater.

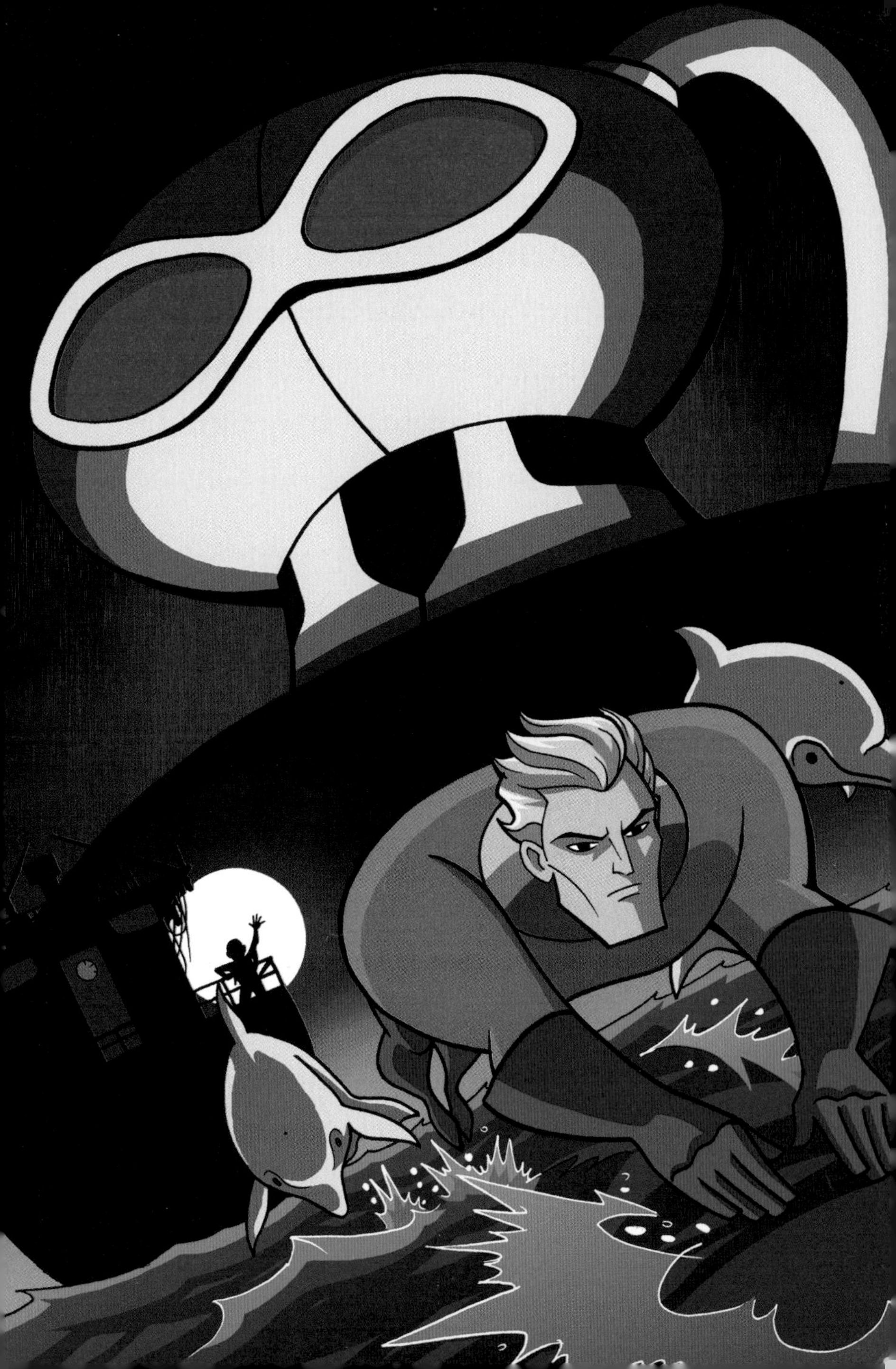

Luckily, he was a skilled inventor. Before long he was swimming the seas in a black waterproof suit. The suit allowed him to pull oxygen from the water and it kept his body warm. It had jet feet and tiny torpedoes and a wide helmet with glowing red eyes. The mask looked like the body of a manta ray.

The boy was no longer himself. He had become Black Manta.

Now, Black Manta watched the octopuses wriggle in the water. Every one of them wore a special black suit like his. The suits were made of strong, stretchy material, which protected them like armor. The suits covered the octopuses' heads and arms, but left their tiny suction cups exposed. This allowed the creatures to move normally and use their jet propulsion.

They could still shoot black ink to confuse an enemy. The suit also allowed them to squeeze through tiny spaces.

Black Manta's red eyes glowed. During their invasion of Atlantis, he'd use his infrared vision a lot.

Black Manta had added another weapon to the black suits. Each one had tiny jets that shot out another black ink, one that put enemies to sleep on contact. During their invasion of Atlantis, they'd be using a lot of that as well.

The octopuses wriggled, waiting for their master to speak. Black Manta pressed the button on his communicator. "It is time," he told them, "for you to take your rightful place in the sea, and for you to have a city of your own. Time for our invasion of Atlantis to begin!"

CHAPTER 2

STEALTH MISSION

Black Manta folded his muscled arms across his chest and eyed the giant octopus in front of him. His name was Ocho. He was the largest octopus in the army. His tentacles were as big as fire hoses. His eyes were as big as Black Manta's fists.

Ocho treaded water easily, moving his appendages so slightly that he looked like he wasn't moving at all. Twice as big as Black Manta himself, the octopus was the stronger creature, but Black Manta had taken extra care to train him.

Ocho was the most obedient octopus in the army. There was a very good reason for this. Ocho wasn't like the rest of octopuses Black Manta had captured. He was stronger. He was faster. He was smarter.

But, in fact, he wasn't an octopus at all. Ocho was Black Manta's best invention ever — an octopus robot. No one knew this, not even the other octopuses. Ocho looked and smelled like a real octopus. He was so much like a real octopus that sometimes even Black Manta forgot that he wasn't.

"You're an excellent student, Ocho," Black Manta said. "Which is why I have chosen you. You will be the second leader of the invasion. It is not an easy job, but I know you can do it. I know you *will* do it."

Ocho calmly treaded water, his black eyes staring into Black Manta's red ones.

After a few moments, Ocho saluted his master with two tentacles. He understood and accepted the challenge.

Black Manta and Ocho swam past a large holding tank. The octopuses inside bobbed silently, waiting for instructions. They would have to be patient.

The next tank was smaller, and only half full. "You are the lead group," Black Manta told a pod of twenty-four octopuses. "Together we will begin the invasion. It will be just as we have planned, as we have practiced. While some of you guard the entrance, others will penetrate. We will travel in the black of night. The people of Atlantis will not hear us. They will not see us. They will not know what hit them . . . until it is too late."

Black Manta turned to the huge octopus by his side. "Ocho is second in command," he said. "He is your leader whenever I am not with you. You are to follow his instructions and obey his orders. Do not question him."

The octopuses wriggled their tentacles and bobbed their heads. Black Manta reached out and unlocked the tank door. In a mass, the octopuses swam out of the hideout and toward the gates of Atlantis.

Black Manta led his octopus army toward the underwater city. He had waited a long time for this day to come. Pushing a button on his wrist, he activated the GPS systems. Built into every octopus suit was a tracking device. The octopuses did not know that they were being traced wherever they went.

With the device, Black Manta would know immediately if one of the octopuses strayed, and he would act quickly.

Just outside the city, the two dozen octopuses got into neat rows. Black Manta and Ocho swam up and down the formation to make sure everyone was ready. Then Black Manta nodded his alien-like head. The first two black-suited creatures swam ahead, moving slowly toward the gate. One swam awkwardly, pretending to be hurt.

"Who are you?" questioned a guard.

Another guard spoke in a soft voice. "Whoever he is, he's injured and needs help." He moved forward through the water, his arms outstretched.

Suddenly, the octopus shot forward.

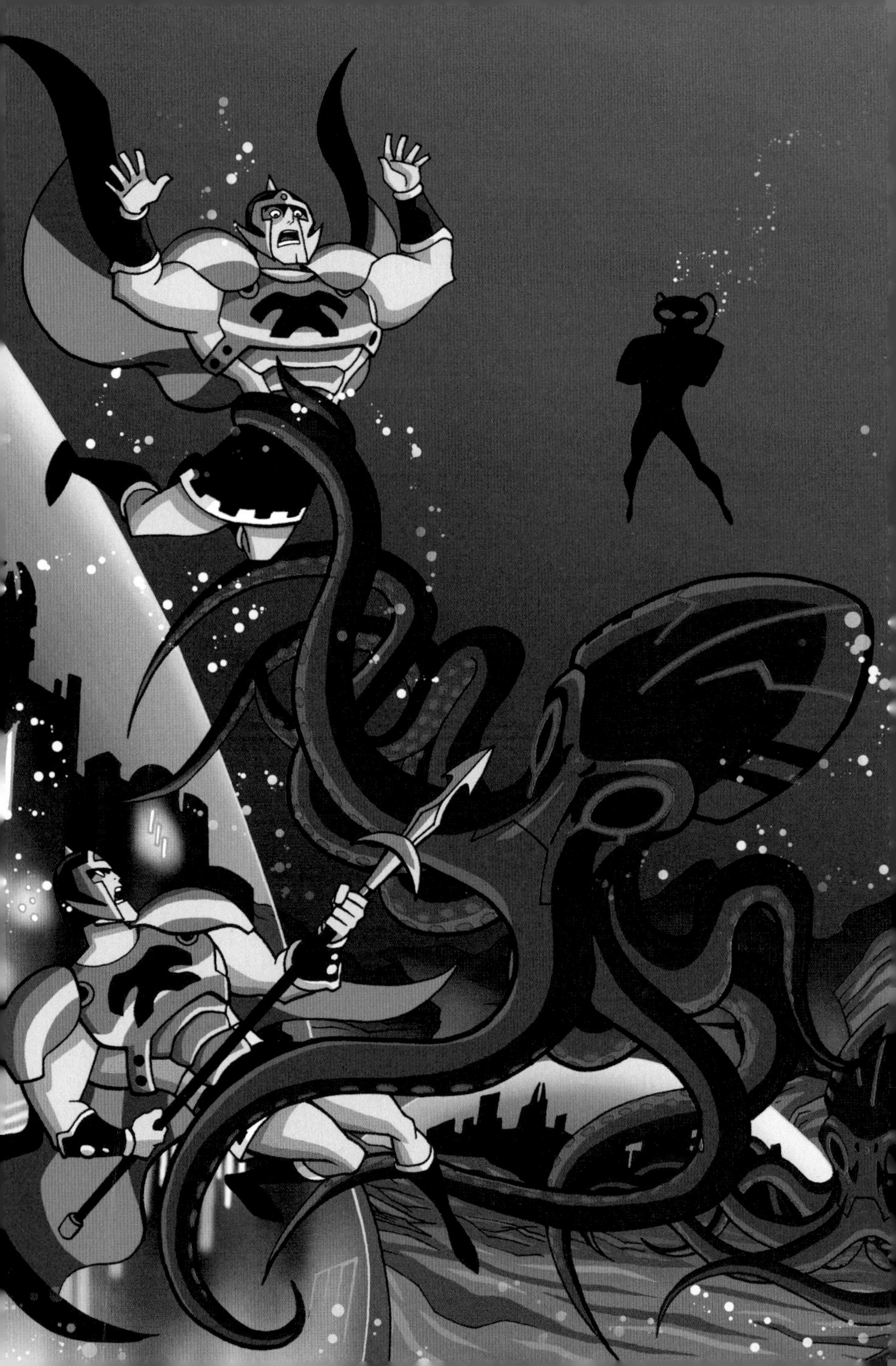

The sea creature wrapped its powerful tentacles around the man. "What?" the man shouted, trying to wriggle free.

The octopus held him tight, being careful not to suffocate the man. They had been instructed to imprison but not to kill. Black Manta wanted the Atlanteans to see their city crumble, and then he would force them to rebuild it.

"Let go of him!" the other man shouted. The second octopus bolted forward, black ink shooting out of its suit. Within seconds, the water was dark and murky.

"I can't see!" cried one of the men, reaching out blindly. Exactly ten seconds later, the first guard went limp in the octopus's arms. The second one flailed, and went still as well.

A short distance away, Black Manta's eyes gleamed. He had spent a long time creating the "ink," building it into the suits and training his subjects to use it. At first, they got confused and squirted their own ink by mistake. Their ink was useful in its own way — it clouded the water and confused enemies. The formula for Black Manta's ink included a powerful drug that would put most species into a deep sleep.

Black Manta grinned wickedly at the limp Atlantean in the octopus's arms. Step one was complete. So far his plan was going swimmingly. Now, the time had come for step two.

"Teams two and three, you're in," Black Manta ordered. Two pairs of octopuses swam gracefully up to the gates. Ocho followed.

The "wounded" octopus now held both Atlanteans in two arms — and still had six free. Teams two and three swam silently through the gates toward the Atlantis History Museum.

Inside the museum, Atlanteans were enjoying the exhibits. The black octopuses moved so silently they were invisible. While Atlanteans chatted, black ink seeped into the water. Moments later, the exhibit area was filled with floating, sleeping bodies.

Ocho used his massive tentacles to force open one of the enclosed exhibits. In a matter of minutes, the Atlanteans were trapped inside their own display.

Ocho pressed several buttons on his communication device. *Museum infiltrated,* was the message he sent to Black Manta.

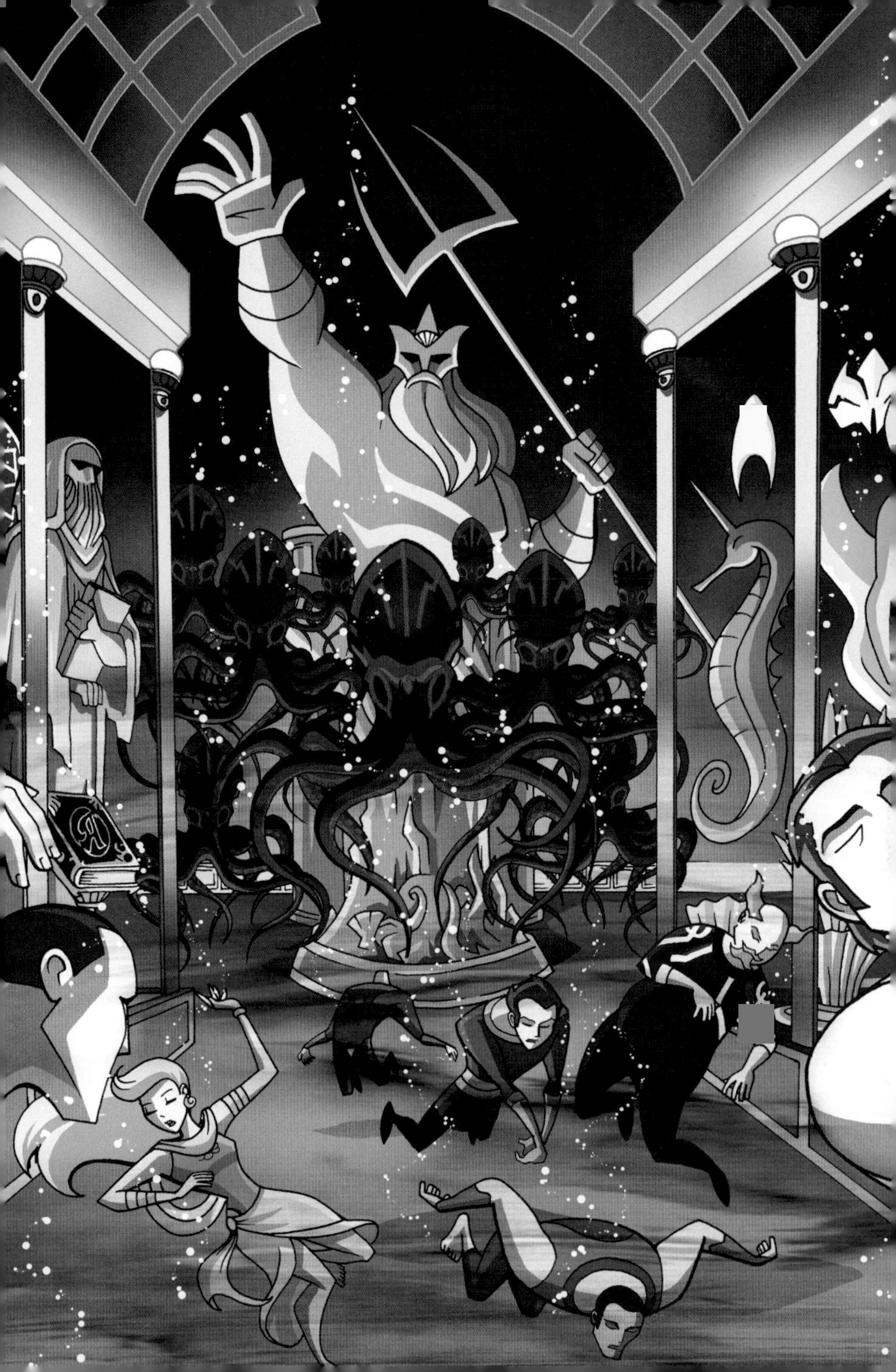

"Excellent," Black Manta said. "I am sending in the remainder of the infiltrators. Atlantis as we know it will be gone before morning."

CHAPTER 3

ATTACK ON ATLANTIS

Black Manta's army moved quickly through the city. In countless surprise attacks, they overtook their victims with poison ink. Other octopuses squeezed into aqueducts and traveled to far corners of the city. Still others moved boldly but quietly down the city's streets.

The octopuses formed barricades outside stores and homes. They captured Atlanteans, easily containing them in their many arms. They filled the water with blackness.

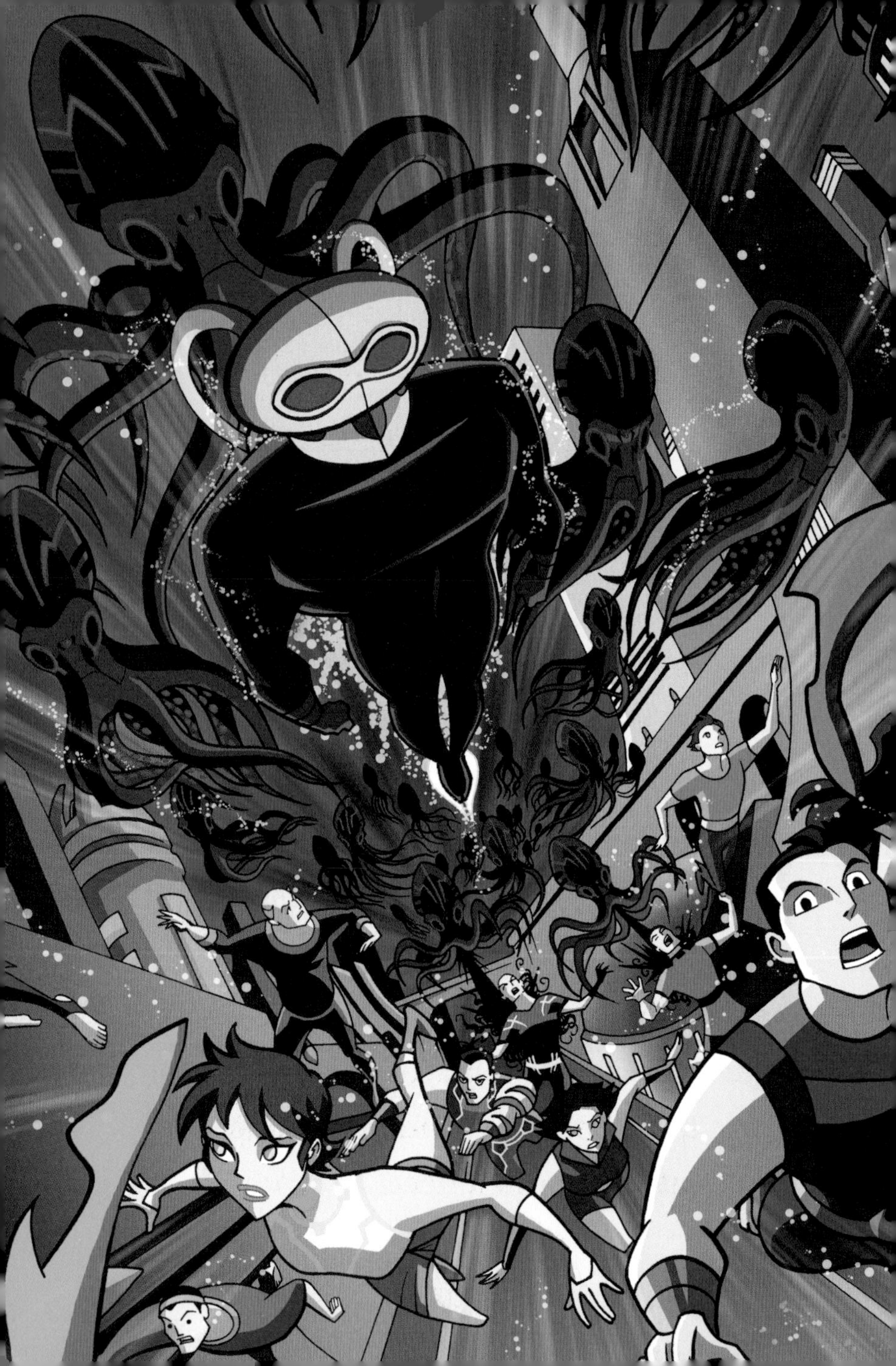

Some Atlanteans tried to flee and some surrendered in fear. Still others fought bravely. None, however, were able to outswim or outfight the creatures or the ink that made everything go black.

A team of transporter octopuses swept over the city. They carried limp victims to the museum, dumping them into the displays. When these holding cells became too full, they dragged their victims to the caverns outside the city. Little by little, Atlantis became an underwater ghost town. By the early hours of the morning, the streets and buildings were empty.

Black Manta kept close tabs on his army and its progress. His army had done well. There was only one place where people were still unaware of what was happening. One place left to conquer . . .

The Royal Palace.

The city is clear, Master, Ocho communicated. *We are ready for you.*

Black Manta sighed. At last, the moment had come. One final attack, and the city would be his. The sea would be his. Aquaman would be gone, and he would be king!

CHAPTER 4

CAPTURING THE KING

In the darkness of his hideout, Black Manta prepared for battle. "The time has come to overtake the palace," he told his octopuses. He opened the doors and a hundred black-suited creatures formed lines behind him. "Follow me."

The sea was completely quiet. Black Manta swam swiftly without making a sound. Atlantis spread out before him, an empty city of darkness. The super-villain's glowing eyes made a red path, helping him see in the ink-stained water.

Ocho met him at the edge of the city. Together, they swam toward the palace with Black Manta's army behind them.

"Attack the palace carefully," Black Manta instructed. "I will handle King Aquaman myself, but I want the guards contained before I enter."

Ocho understood. He swam forward, leading the octopuses through the gates. When Black Manta entered the courtyard minutes later, eight palace guards were hanging limp in Ocho's muscular arms.

"Dispose of them as you see fit," Black Manta said. Ocho nodded and carried the guards into the darkness.

Black Manta stared up at the palace, his red eyes narrowing. Then he and his army pressed forward. "Onward!" he shouted.

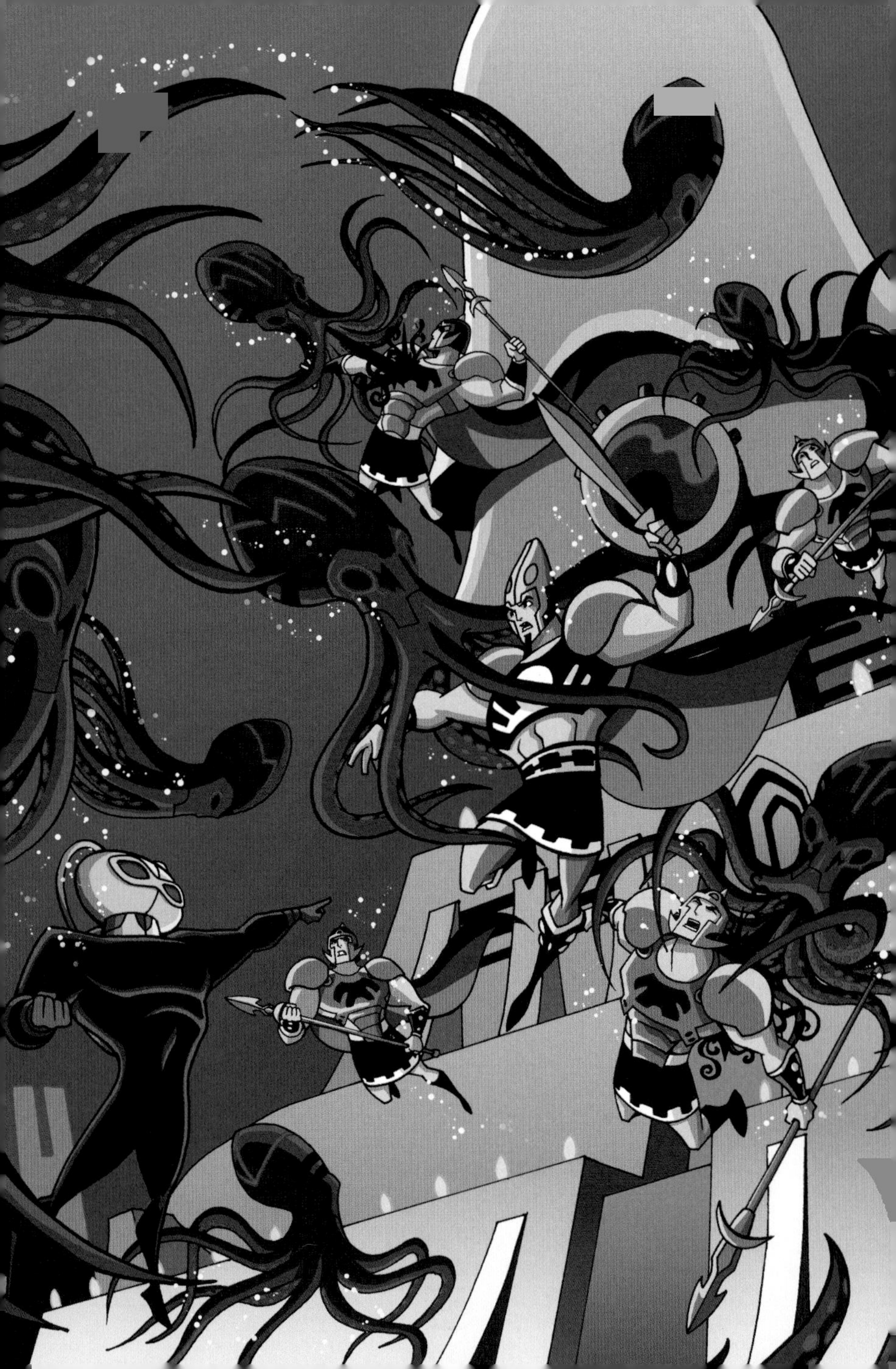

Several large octopuses moved in front of him and hurled themselves at the massive palace door. It shattered. The super-villain easily swam through the broken barrier.

A long line of guards and castle workers waited in the great hall. They were armed with knives, spears, and swords. They looked ready to fight.

"Half of you take care of them," Black Manta ordered. "The other half, follow me. If you can keep up," he added with a chuckle. He pressed a button on his suit and rocketed up the stairs, bursting through a door into Aquaman's quarters.

"Aquaman," he bellowed at the sleeping leader. "Wake up! Your reign as king of Atlantis is over."

Aquaman bolted upright in bed.

The Sea King looked around the room in a panic. "W-what —?" he sputtered. "What's going on?"

"You're surrendering," Black Manta replied. "To me."

A pair of octopuses grabbed Aquaman's arms and legs. They wrapped their remaining tentacles around his torso.

Black Manta couldn't believe how easy this was!

But before the octopuses could take Aquaman away, a familiar voice thundered through the chamber.

"Hello, Manta."

Black Manta shook his head in confusion. His dark heart skipped a beat. He knew that voice.

Black Manta hated that voice, and he hated the man who owned it even more.

Aquaman.

But if Aquaman was standing in front of him, who was sleeping in his bed?

"A decoy, of course." Aquaman answered the question Black Manta hadn't asked. Black Manta's heart filled with hatred as he stared at Aquaman. The king repulsed him in every way. Aquaman had betrayed him. He had left him to suffer on that ship long ago. More than anything, Black Manta longed to destroy him.

"How nice of you to be waiting for me," Black Manta said with a sneer.

Aquaman shook his mane of yellow hair. "Black Manta," he said. "I should have known it was you."

Black Manta's eyes gleamed. "Is anyone else capable of such a silent invasion?"

"Invasion?" Aquaman repeated.

"Yes, and a successful one, too," Black Manta boasted. "Your citizens have been moved into the museum. Your guards are being held captive in your own dungeons. Your beloved city has been seized."

Aquaman sighed. "I commend you, Black Manta. But tell me, why do you want Atlantis?"

Black Manta threw back his head and howled with laughter. "How like you to only see part of the picture," he said. "Atlantis is simply a stepping stone, a starting point. The captured Atlanteans will help me build it into a great empire from which I will rule the seas!"

"They'll never help you!" Aquaman stepped closer, his blue eyes flashing.

"Your people will work for me and do my bidding," Black Manta hissed. "If they do not, they will remain prisoners, trapped as I was on that ship many years ago."

"I did not hear you call for me!" Aquaman protested. He had told Black Manta this many times.

"You were a hundred feet away, and the seas were calm," Black Manta replied. "Even as a young boy, I had a strong voice. You left me there on purpose!"

Aquaman sighed. It was no use — Black Manta would never believe him.

"Still, I am happy to see you," Black Manta said. "Capturing the king is an essential part of my plan."

He snapped his fingers and Ocho sprang from the shadows, grabbing Aquaman by the shoulders and holding him tight.

Aquaman allowed himself to be held. He calmly turned his head to look the octopus in the eye. "What are you doing?"

Ocho stared blankly at Aquaman.

"Have you turned against the sea?" Aquaman went on. "Have you forgotten your fellow ocean species? Your friends, the Atlanteans?"

Ocho made no sign of understanding.

Black Manta's eyes gleamed. "Don't bother trying to communicate with Ocho," he said. "He is not one of your kind."

Aquaman squirmed in the giant octopus's massive arms. "What is he?" he asked quietly.

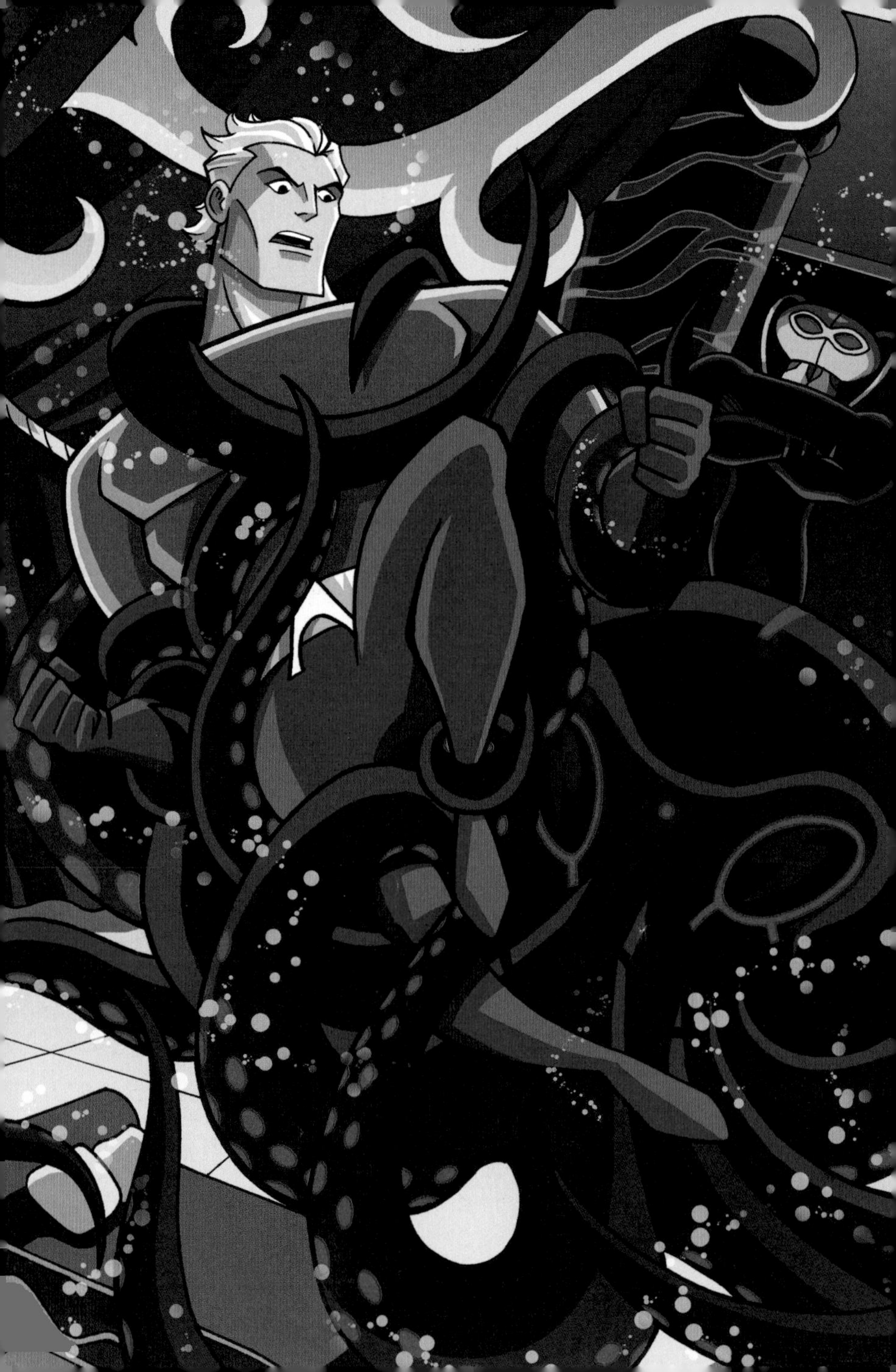

"A brilliant creation that only I control."

Aquaman shook his head.

"So that's it?" Black Manta asked. "You're just going to give in? How disappointing. I was really hoping for more of a challenge."

The king's chambers were completely silent. Black Manta and Aquaman stared at one another. The water around them began to quiver. It vibrated. And then, in a massive rush, sea creatures of every size, shape, color, and kind swarmed into the king's chambers. Aquaman's army had come to rescue him.

Ocho let go of the Sea King. In a flash, he was out of reach.

"Catch him!" Black Manta cried as Aquaman swam through a window.

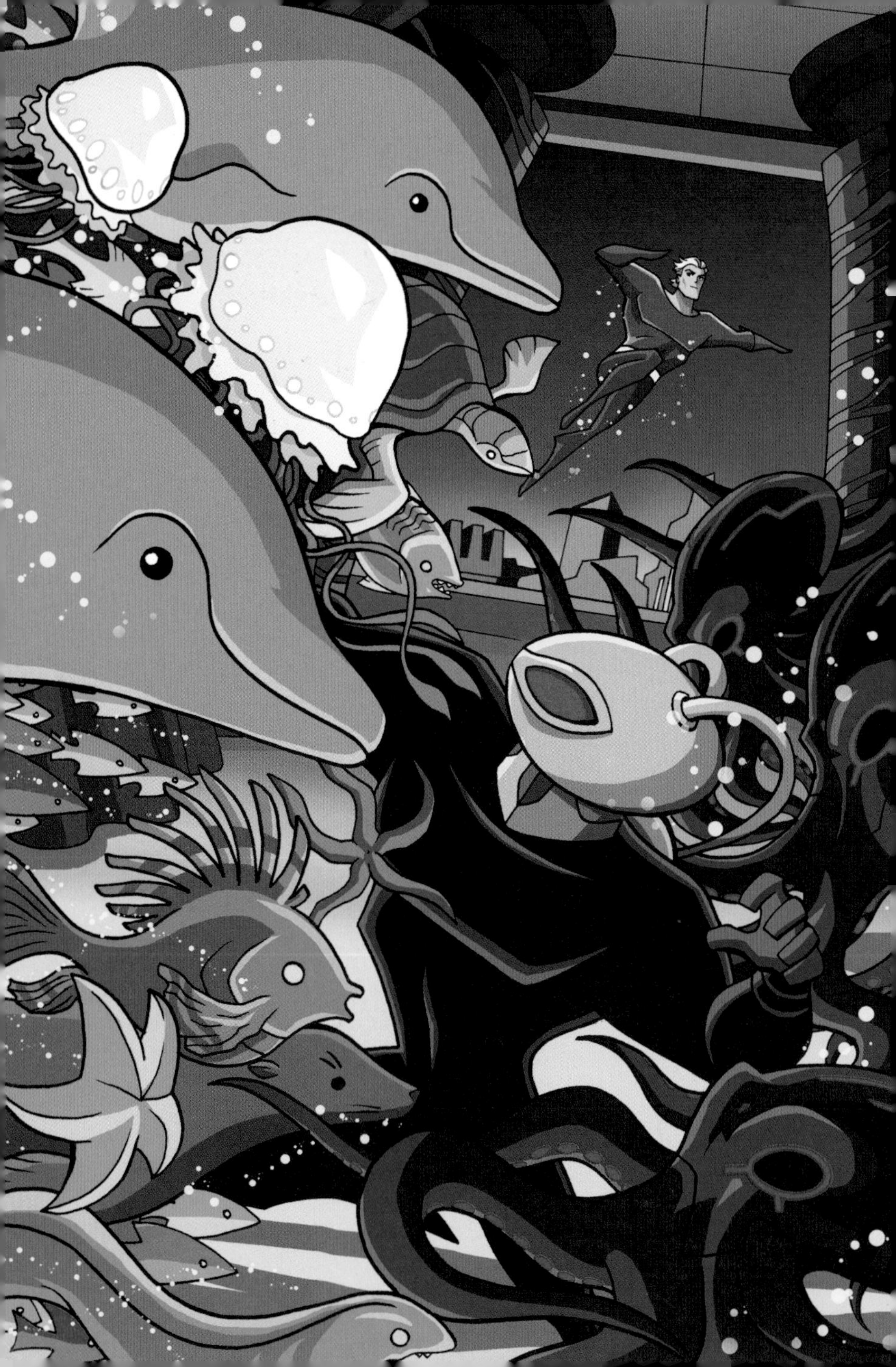

"Follow him!" the super-villain cried out. "Stop him! Defeat him!"

Black Manta's army divided into two groups. Half stayed to fight the army of sea creatures. The other half swarmed through the window after Aquaman.

Aquaman was fast. He also had the advantage of knowing Atlantis better than anyone.

In the king's chambers, Black Manta fumed while his octopuses grabbed at the sea creatures with their many arms. The creatures were slippery! The jellyfish were especially hard to catch, and their stings were painful.

"You fool!" Black Manta shouted. "You let him go!"

Ocho stared blankly at his master. *But you said you wanted a challenge,* he communicated. *Capturing him a second time should not be any harder.*

Black Manta threatened, "I hope not . . . for your sake."

CHAPTER 5

THE REAL ENEMY

Black Manta and Ocho swam through the streets of Atlantis. The super-villain's red eyes cast an eerie glow on the buildings. All around him black-suited octopuses battled Aquaman's sea creatures, and they were gaining the upper hand. Black Manta has chosen his army well — eight arms was a lot to fight against.

Suddenly, Black Manta's communicator beeped. "They've spotted Aquaman," he told Ocho. "He's in a cave on the west side of the city."

Black Manta knew that part of Atlantis, and the caves that ran along one side of it. "Clever," he murmured as he kicked harder. Fortunately, it wasn't far away. "Stay close and don't do anything stupid," he told Ocho. "I wouldn't want this to be your last day in the sea."

Ocho stiffened but silently kept up, his tentacles propelling him through the water.

Up ahead, the mouth of a big cave loomed like a giant maw. Black Manta did a smooth dolphin kick and moved faster. But just as he approached the opening, a mass of sea creatures spewed out. Black Manta batted them away as best he could, but there were thousands of them. And many were too small to see clearly.

"Use your ink!" he shouted to Ocho.

Ocho's black eyes were unblinking. *I don't have ink,* he communicated.

Black Manta's antenna flicked with rage. The robot octopus was right. He didn't have ink! Black Manta had forgotten to equip his creation with this poison. Only the suited octopuses had it.

Black Manta pushed a button on his communication device. "Backup to the west quadrant of the city. NOW!" he ordered.

Within seconds, a large squad of octopuses arrived. Black Manta ordered them to spread their toxic ink, but they refused.

"They're not listening!" Black Manta bellowed.

"Of course not," Aquaman replied, appearing from the cave. "Most sea creatures are engineered to live together in harmony. They will fight only their known enemies."

"You!" Black Manta shrieked. "You are the enemy!" He pressed another button, activating his jet pack. He charged Aquaman, smashing him against the rock next to the cave opening.

Bouncing off the wall, Aquaman raised his legs and shoved Black Manta all the way to the other side of the street. *Oomf!*

"No, Black Manta, *you* are the enemy. You have captured these poor creatures and brainwashed them to do your evil bidding."

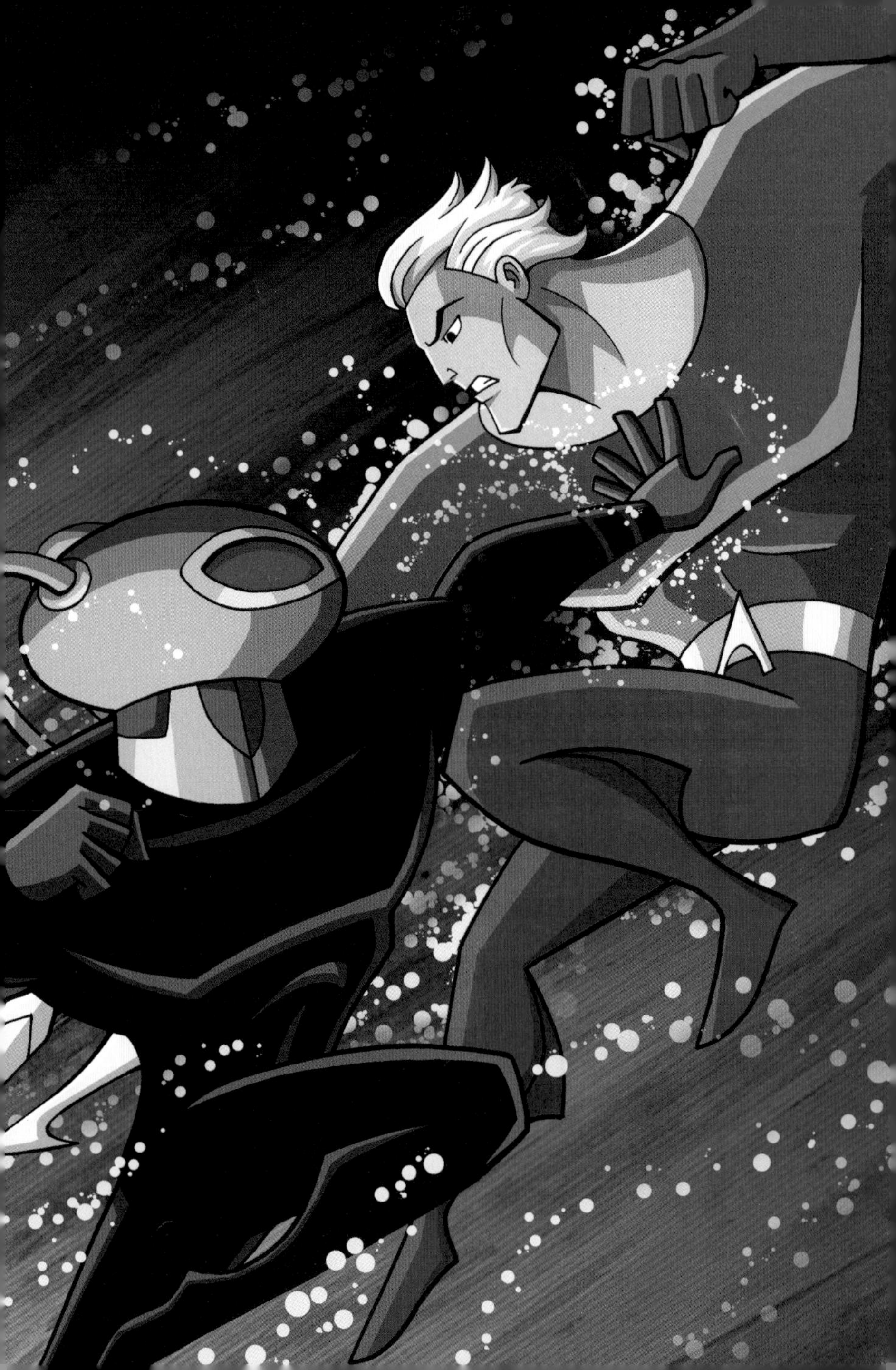

In a rage, Black Manta drew his spear and flew toward Aquaman, hurling his weapon at his enemy's chest.

Aquaman ducked and the spear struck an octopus, cutting right through the black suit and into its soft flesh. The octopus slumped to the seafloor.

Black Manta ignored the injured octopus. He had hundreds more! But he did not notice that his army was staring at him, their dark eyes filled with anger.

"Capture him!" Black Manta shouted, pointing at Aquaman.

But they didn't. Instead, an octopus gently picked up its wounded friend and held it close.

"Ocho! Take him!" Black Manta ordered.

Ocho did not move.

He calmly treaded water as if he could not understand what Black Manta was saying. And then, all at once, the octopuses wriggled themselves out of their black suits. Their natural, brightly colored bodies glimmered in the dim light.

"What are you doing?" Black Manta gasped.

"Becoming themselves," Aquaman replied. "Your attempt to brainwash these creatures and take over Atlantis has failed."

Two octopuses carried their friend off to receive treatment while the others closed in on their new enemy. Black Manta only had one choice. Hitting a button on his suit, he jetted himself to safety.

ZOOOM!

As he zoomed up and out of Atlantis, his voice echoed down to Aquaman and the octopus. "This isn't over, Aquaman!" he howled. "One day I will put an end to you . . . once and for all!"

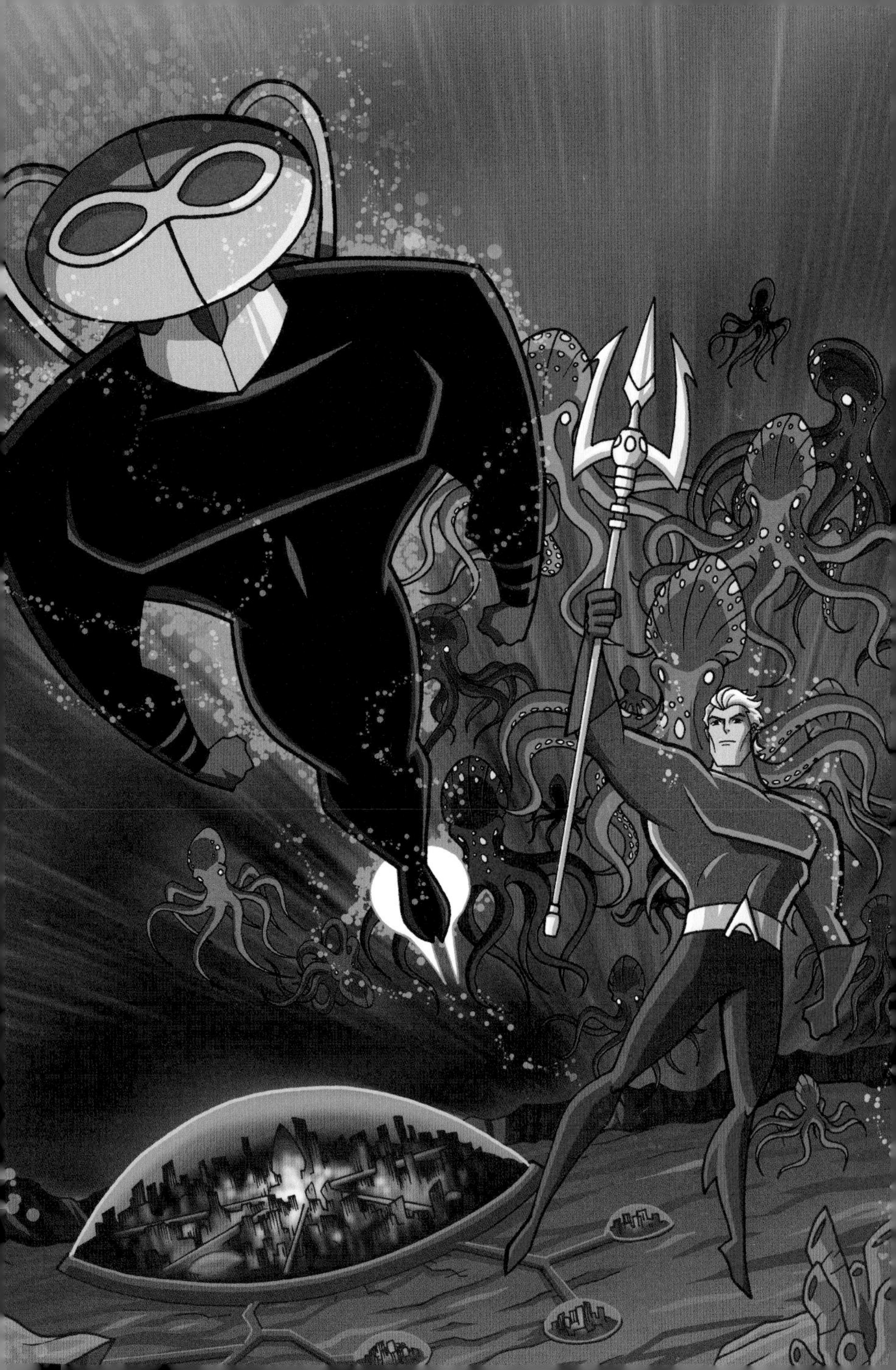

BIOGRAPHIES

Jane Mason is no super hero, but having three kids sometimes makes her wish she had superpowers. Jane has written children's books for more than fifteen years and hopes to continue doing so for fifty more. She makes her home in Oakland, California, with her husband, three children, their dog, and a gecko.

Luciano Vecchio was born in 1982 and currently lives in Buenos Aires, Argentina. With experience in illustration, animation and comics, his works have been published in the US, Spain, UK, France and Argentina. Credits include Ben 10 (DC Comics), Cruel Thing (Norma), Unseen Tribe (Zuda Comics) and Sentinels (Drumfish Productions).

GLOSSARY

appendage (uh-PEN-dij)—an arm, leg, tentacle, or other type of limb

Atlantis (at-LAN-tiss)—a island kingdom said to have sunk beneath the sea long ago

brainwashed (BRAYN-wahshd)—made someone accept and believe something by saying it over and over again

brilliant (BRIL-ee-uhnt)—very smart, or splendid and terrific

infiltrated (IN-fil-trate-id)—snuck in somewhere without anyone noticing

invasion (in-VAY-zhuhn)—a coordinated attack on an enemy by a group of attackers

obedient (oh-BEE-dee-uhnt)—if you are obedient, you do what you're told to do

propulsion (pruh-PUHL-shuhn)—the force by which something is pushed along

specimens (SPESS-uh-muhnz)—samples or examples used to stand for a whole group

vowed (VOUD)—made a serious and important promise

DISCUSSION QUESTIONS

1. Some people believe that the lost underwater city of Atlantis really exists. What do you think?

2. Why do you think Black Manta and Aquaman don't get along? Could these enemies ever become friends? How?

3. This book has ten illustrations. Which one is your favorite? Why?

WRITING PROMPTS

1. Black Manta trains sea creatures to follow his orders. If you could have an animal as a pet, what kind of animal would you choose? What would its name be? Write about your new pet, and then draw a picture of it.

2. Rewrite the final chapter of this book from Aquaman's perspective. What does he think of Black Manta? What will he do now?

3. What evil scheme does Black Manta think up next? Write about it.

THE FUN DOESN'T STOP HERE!
DISCOVER MORE AT...
WWW.CAPSTONEKIDS.COM
GAMES & PUZZLES
VIDEOS & CONTESTS
HEROES & VILLAINS
AUTHORS & ILLUSTRATORS
FIND COOL WEBSITES AND MORE BOOKS LIKE THIS ONE AT WWW.FACTHOUND.COM.
JUST TYPE IN THE BOOK ID: 9781434226259 AND YOU'RE READY TO GO!

LOOK FOR MORE

SUPER DC ~~HEROES~~ VILLAINS

LEX LUTHOR AND THE
KRYPTONITE CAVERNS

SINESTRO AND THE
RING OF FEAR

CHEETAH AND THE
PURRFECT CRIME

JOKER ON THE
HIGH SEAS

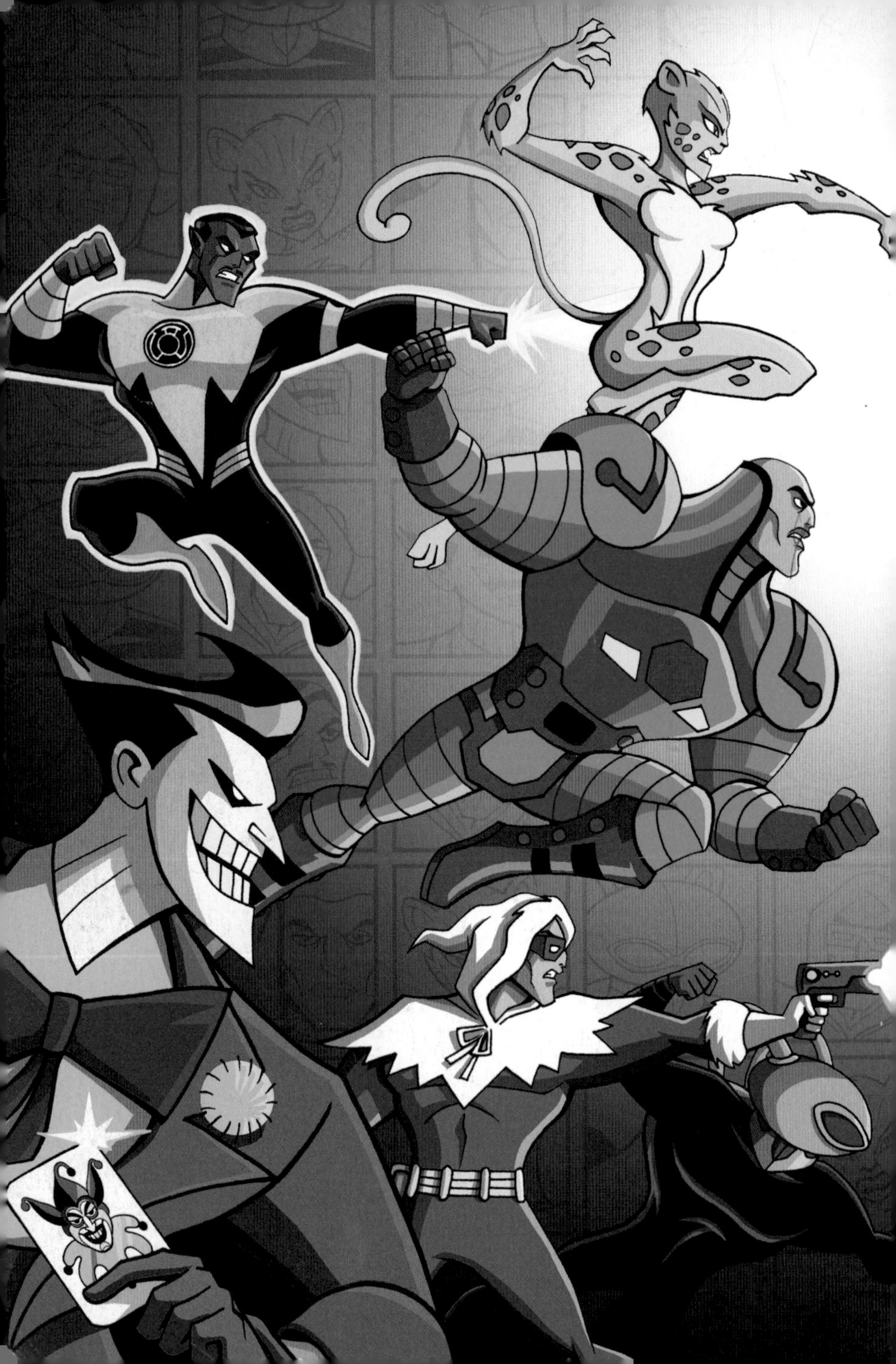

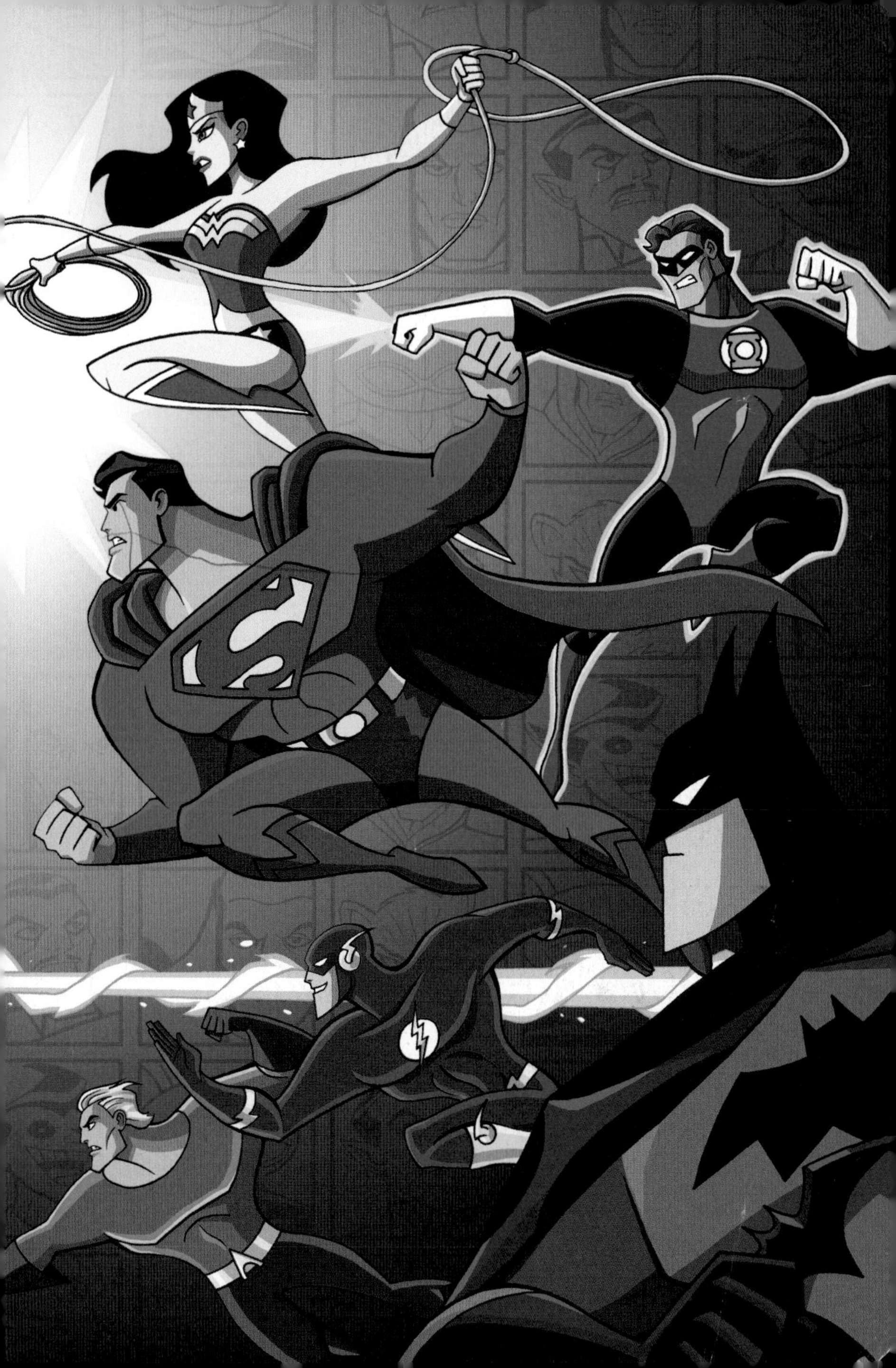

SUPER DC™ ~~HEROES~~ -VILLAINS